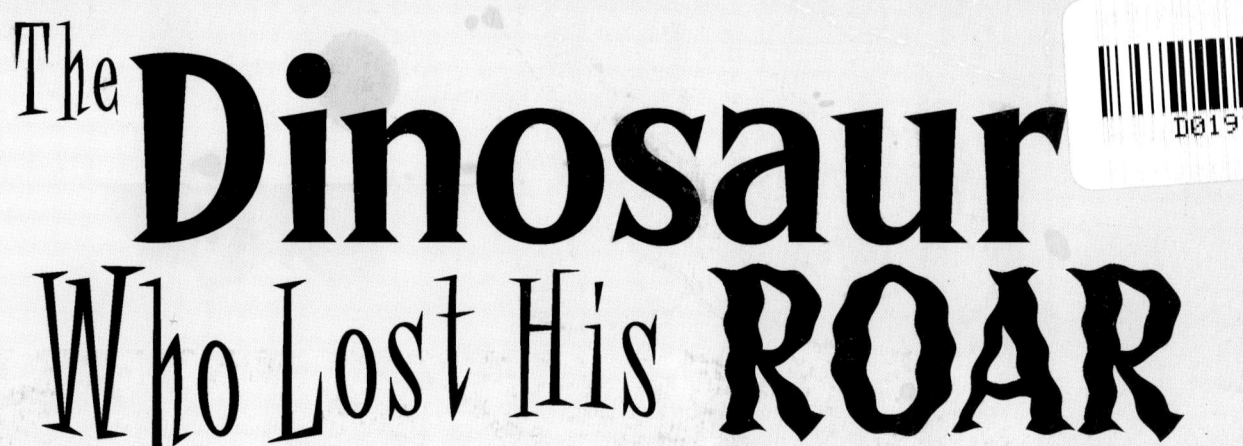

The Dinosaur Who Lost His ROAR

Russell Punter

Illustrated by Andy Elkerton

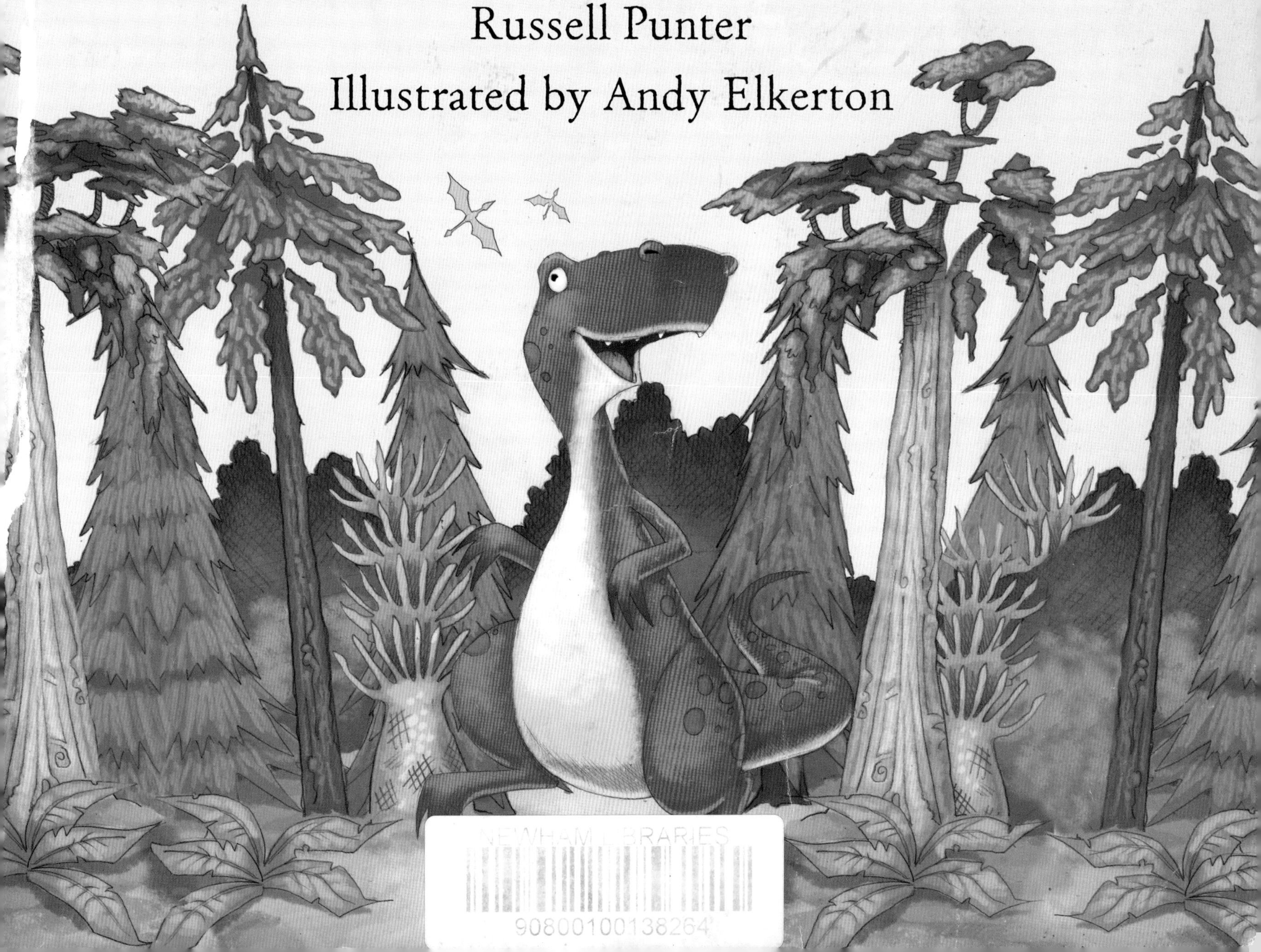

Deep inside the forest,
lived a dinosaur named Sid.

ROAR!

He always got in trouble
for the noisy things he did.

Spike was picking berries,

Sid crept up like a cat.

He let out such a mighty **ROAR!**

...that Spike got covered. SPLAT!

"That wasn't funny, Sid," growled Spike.

"The juice went in my eyes."

"Enjoy your breakfast!" Sid replied.

"Who else can I surprise?"

Ross was standing by the pool
to see what he could catch.

When Sid let out a mighty **ROAR!**

...poor Ross went tumbling. SPLASH!

"I hope you liked your swim, Ross. You'll dry out in the end."

"That wasn't funny," Ross replied. "I thought you were my friend."

Sid saw Ellie hunting eggs.

He sneaked behind her back.

He let out such a mighty

ROAR!

...the eggs went
flying. CRACK!

"An eggs-ellent surprise," laughed Sid.
"You just can't beat my roar."

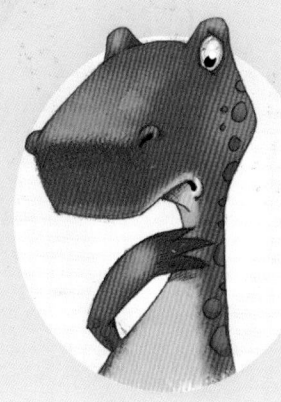

But when he went to bed that night,
his throat felt rough and sore.

The next day, Sid saw Spike again
and went to play his joke.

But when he tried to give a roar,
what came out
was a...

croak!

"Ha ha, Sid. You've lost your roar.
You can't scare me any more."

Ross was balanced on a rock. Sid went to scare him off.
But when he tried to give a roar,
what came out
was a...

cough!

"Ha ha, Sid. You've lost your roar.
You can't scare me any more."

Sid tiptoed up to Ellie,
but struggle though he might,

no roar would come out

– just a rasp...

His throat felt oh-so tight.

raaasssp!

"Ha ha, Sid. You've lost your roar.
You can't scare me any more."

Sid spent a whole week
getting well,

with honey
and sweet tea.

"Oh, I wish I hadn't
played those tricks.

Now the

joke's on me."

Soon Sid felt fit
to see his friends.

"I'll show them
I'm not mean."

But when he reached
the berry bush,
Spike could not be seen.

Ross was missing
from his pool,

Sid sensed that things weren't right.

He spotted scary footprints
and they gave him quite a fright.

Sid was getting worried.

What would he come to next?

Then came a shock, beyond a rock –

Tyrannosaurus Rex!

Sid hoped he had his voice back.

But how could he be sure?

He took the most enormous breath,

and gave a mighty...

The T-Rex headed for the hills.

Sid's pals were safe once more.

"Three cheers for Sid the hero,

You're the **greatest** dinosaur!"

(And what became of bad T-Rex?

Well, he was seen no more...

He just kept right on running,
still scared by Sid's great ROAR!)

Edited by Jenny Tyler and Lesley Sims

First published in 2012 by Usborne Publishing Ltd., Usborne House, 83-85 Saffron Hill, London EC1N 8RT, England. www.usborne.com
Copyright © 2012 Usborne Publishing Ltd.